DEVELOPING READER
LEVEL 2
250-750 WORDS

Six Rainbow Magic Stories!

The Rainbow Fairies
The Fairies' Birthday Surprise
Best Friends in Fairyland
A Fairy Ballet
The Fairy Treasure Hunt
A Fairyland Costume Ball

By Daisy Meadows

SCHOLASTIC INC.

To Wilson, who fills each day with color

With special thanks to Kristin Earhart

The Rainbow Fairies

Amber the Orange Fairy

Sky the Blue Fairy

Fern the Green Fairy

Sunny the Yellow Fairy

Ruby the Red Fairy

Heather the Violet Fairy

Inky the Indigo Fairy

The Rainbow Fairies (978-0-545-22291-4) Copyright © 2010 by Rainbow Magic Limited.
The Fairies' Birthday Surprise (978-0-545-22292-1) Copyright © 2010 by Rainbow Magic Limited.
Best Friends in Fairyland (978-0-545-22293-8) Copyright © 2010 by Rainbow Magic Limited.
A Fairy Ballet (978-0-545-22294-5) Copyright © 2011 by Rainbow Magic Limited.
The Fairy Treasure Hunt (978-0-545-38493-3) Copyright © 2012 by Rainbow Magic Limited.
A Fairyland Costume Ball (978-0-545-43389-1) Copyright © 2012 by Rainbow Magic Limited.

12 11 10 9 8 7 6 5 4 3 2 1   13 14 15 16 17 18/0

Printed in Singapore   46
This edition first printing, June 2013

The Rainbow Fairies

By Daisy Meadows

It is a special day in Fairyland.
Today is the Feast of All Colors,
so the Fairy King and Queen
are having a picnic to celebrate.

YOU ARE
INVITED TO
The Feast
of All
Colors

All the fairies are excited, especially
the Rainbow Fairies.

Inky
the Indigo
Fairy

Amber
the Orange
Fairy

Fern
the Green
Fairy

Sunny
the Yellow
Fairy

They get to choose the foods for the picnic.
There are seven Rainbow Fairies, one
for each color of the rainbow.

Ruby
the Red
Fairy

Heather
the Violet
Fairy

Sky
the Blue
Fairy

They are sisters, and they share an
important job:
to fill the world with color!

The Rainbow Fairies are busy in
their toadstool cottage.
It is almost time to fill the picnic baskets.

Just then, the fairy sisters
hear a knock at the door.

"Hello, Rainbow Fairies," a voice croaks.

"Bertram!" the sisters exclaim.

Bertram the frog is a royal messenger and also their good friend.

"The king asked me to clean your
wands," says Bertram.

"Of course," Ruby replies.

"They need to work well for the feast,"
Inky agrees.

The fairies hand their wands to Bertram,
who wipes them with a magic cloth.
As the fairies talk about the foods they will
pick, Bertram's stomach growls.

"Excuse me," says the frog.
"I can't wait for the picnic!
The food will be delicious!"

Bertram returns the wands to
the fairies, one by one.

But he isn't thinking about wands,
he is thinking about the feast.

"Thank you, Bertram," the fairies say.

"I am happy to help!" he replies.

"I'll see you at the picnic!"

The fairies carry the empty picnic baskets
outside to the meadow.
"What a beautiful day for a picnic!" Fern
exclaims.

"But it isn't a picnic without food,"
insists Sunny.
Heather says, "Let's get started!"

"I'll go first," says Ruby.
She thinks of her favorite red foods.

"Strawberries, tomatoes, and cherries!" Ruby says.

Sparkles stream from her wand into one of the picnic baskets.

Now it's Amber's turn.

She flicks her wand.

"Sweet potatoes, carrots, and tangerines!" she calls out.

"I'm next," says Sunny.

"Corn on the cob with butter! And
lemonade!"

Sparkles stream into the basket.

"Now for green," Fern says. "Broccoli, peas,
and cool cucumber soup, please!"

"Blueberry pie!" Sky declares happily.

"Blackberries!" sings Inky.

"Grape jelly!" exclaims Heather.

Sparkles fly from their wands and spin through the air.

"Hooray!" cry the fairies. "The picnic is
ready!"
"Let's go home and wash up before the feast,"
Ruby says.

Just as the fairies leave, someone arrives early for the feast.

It's Bertram, and he's hungry!
He tiptoes up to a picnic basket, lifts the
cover, and looks inside.
"Oh, no!" he cries.

Ruby rushes out of the cottage. "What's the matter, Bertram?"

Bertram points to the baskets and Ruby looks inside.

"Red corn on the cob? Blue strawberries? Violet tangerines?" she mumbles.

"What went wrong?" Bertram asks. "That food does not look delicious."

Ruby's eyes grow wide. "We must have used the wrong wands!" she realizes. "I have to call my sisters!"

Ruby points her wand straight up and blue sparkles shoot into the air.

Soon, the other Rainbow Fairies return to the meadow.

"We got back the wrong wands after Bertram cleaned them," Ruby explains. "And the picnic foods are all the wrong colors!"
"Can we fix it?" Sky asks.

"We need to work together," Ruby says. "We need Rainbow Magic! And fast! The king and queen are coming!"

At once, the sisters make a circle.

They hold their wands up high and speak
together:
"Rainbow colors, bold and bright,
The picnic foods are just not right.
Now each wand must find its fairy
And fix the shade of each grape and berry."

The wands spin around in the air, and
each one lands in the hand of its fairy.
Just then, sparkles of every color shimmer
and swirl through the meadow.

"What a beautiful beginning to the Feast of
All Colors!" announces the king.
"The food looks delicious," the queen says.

"Yes, it does," agrees Bertram, winking at the
Rainbow Fairies.
Everyone sits down to enjoy a colorful feast.
They have a lot to celebrate!

The Fairies'
Birthday Surprise

To Margaret,
the fairy queen of baking birthday cakes.

And to Katherine,
the royal frosting taster!

With special thanks to Kristin Earhart

The Rainbow Fairies

Amber the Orange Fairy

Sky the Blue Fairy

Fern the Green Fairy

Sunny the Yellow Fairy

Heather the Violet Fairy

Ruby the Red Fairy

Inky the Indigo Fairy

The Fairies'
Birthday Surprise

By Daisy Meadows

A trumpet sounds from Fairyland castle, and the Rainbow Fairies awake.

"Is that the royal trumpet?" Ruby asks.

"Yes, today is the Fairy Queen's birthday!" Sky remembers.

"We should do something special for her," Fern says.

"Let's bake her a cake," Inky says.

"Yes," Sunny agrees. "Let's make it from scratch."

"What does that mean?" Heather asks.

"It means we'll make it by hand," Sunny explains, "and we won't use magic."
The fairy sisters look at one another.
They *always* use magic.

"Making it from scratch is special," Ruby
says. "Let's do it!"

Amber opens a cookbook.

"The recipe calls for sugar, butter, eggs, flour,
baking powder, and milk," she reads aloud.

"We don't have eggs, milk, or butter," she
says, looking up.

"I can make them!" Heather suggests, raising her wand.

"Wait!" declares Sunny. "We all agreed, no magic."

The Rainbow Fairies fly to the Fairyland farm. Ruby, Amber, and Inky head into the henhouse.

"Cluckity cluck," the hens call as the
fairies take eggs from their warm nests.
"Thank you, ladies," Inky says as they leave.

The other fairies are in the cow barn.
"The recipe calls for milk and butter,"
remembers Fern.

"We can churn the milk into butter,"
Heather says.
Sunny and Sky sit down on the stools and
begin to milk.

The fairies put the eggs and milk in a wagon, and Sunny pulls it.

"This is hard work!" she says.

"It would be easier with magic," says Heather.

"But we agreed," Inky insists.

"I know," answers Heather, "no magic."

The fairies return to the cottage.
Ruby and Amber crack the eggs.

Sunny and Fern churn the butter.
Sky, Inky, and Heather mix the batter.
It is messy work!

The fairies pour the batter into seven pans and put them in the oven.

Amber looks at the clock. "The cakes should be done just in time for the party," she says. "We'll clean up while they bake," says Sunny.

Ding!

"They are ready!" Fern declares.

Each fairy pulls a cake from the oven.

They stack the seven cakes and admire their hard work.

"Oh, no!" cries Sunny. "We forgot the icing."

"We don't have time to make icing from scratch," Amber says.

"We worked so hard," Ruby says. "A little magic couldn't hurt."

Sparkles whirl from Ruby's wand and swirl around the cake.

At once, the cake is covered with white icing!

"Now we need to add color," says Ruby.

But the fairies cannot agree on how to
decorate the cake.

Fern says, "The bottom layer should be green,
like grass." She flicks her wand, and green
icing covers the bottom cake.

"No, it should be blue," insists Sky.

All of the fairies want to make the cake
pretty, and each fairy has her own favorite
color.
They all point their wands at the cake at the
same time.
Whoosh! Sparkles spin around the kitchen.

"What's happening?" asks Sky. "The sparkles won't stop."

"Maybe we used too much magic," Inky suggests.

When the sparkles disappear, the fairies
gasp.
The cake is a mess of color.

"What should we do?" Sunny asks. "The party is starting."

"I don't think we should use any more magic," Amber says.

"We baked a cake for the queen," says Inky. "We should give it to her."

The fairy sisters put the cake in their wagon
and pull it to the royal garden.
The party has started, but the crowd grows
quiet as the Rainbow Fairies wheel in
the cake.
The king and queen stand.

"You baked me a cake!" says the Fairy Queen.
Amber cuts a piece and hands it to the queen.

The queen takes a bite. "It's delicious!" she exclaims. "It reminds me of my birthday cakes as a little fairy. My mother and I made them from scratch." She takes another bite.

"Except for the icing. We used a little magic for that." The queen smiles at the sisters. "I love the colorful icing. Only the Rainbow Fairies could have made this cake! It's a real treat."

When they are done serving the guests, the Rainbow Fairies sit down to have some cake, too. "It's wonderful," says Amber.

"It is good," Heather agrees, "but my piece needs more icing." She gives her wand a twirl and a big frosted flower appears. "Yum!" she exclaims. "Now it tastes magical!"

Best Friends
in Fairyland

To Aster and Terefech—the best of friends.

With special thanks to Kristin Earhart

Pearl
the Cloud Fairy

Abigail
the Breeze Fairy

The
Weather
Fairies

Goldie
the Sunshine Fairy

Hayley
the Rain Fairy

Crystal
the Snow Fairy

Storm
the Lightning Fairy

Evie
the Mist Fairy

Best Friends in Fairyland

By Daisy Meadows

It is a brisk fall day in Fairyland.
The Weather Fairies are waiting for
Alabaster, their best friend.
They are going to play their favorite game,
hide-and-seek.

Alabaster is a young unicorn.
He lives with his herd in the
Fairyland Forest.
Alabaster loves to play games with
the Weather Fairies.

The fairies hear a whinny.

"Quick! Hide!" whispers Storm.

Alabaster gallops into the orchard.

"Come out! Come out!" Alabaster calls, stamping his hoof. "Have you heard the news?"

The Weather Fairies peek out from behind the leaves.
"What news?" Hayley asks.

"The Fairy King and Queen are in the forest,"
the unicorn says. "They're picking new
unicorns to lead their carriage."
"Wow!" Crystal exclaims. "That's an honor."
"I bet all the unicorns want to pull the
carriage," Evie adds.

"Yes, my parents are trying out," Alabaster
says. "Do you want to watch?"

"Absolutely!" Goldie exclaims.

"The tryouts are in the clearing," Alabaster says.

"Let's go!" says Storm.

Crystal and Storm fly up ahead, while
the other fairies walk with Alabaster.

The king and queen are already in the
clearing, watching the tryouts.
"My mom and dad are over there," Alabaster
says. He points with his horn.
"Ooooh," Pearl whispers. "They're wonderful."
The two unicorns run side by side and leap
into the air.

The king and queen speak with each pair of unicorns that tried out.

Alabaster and the Weather Fairies wait.

The king and queen talk to each other.
At last, the queen turns to the crowd.
"Our next lead unicorns will be Quicksilver
and Lady Gray," she announces.
Alabaster gasps, "Those are my parents."

The young unicorns gather around Alabaster.
"You get to live in the palace stables," one
unicorn says.
"You're so lucky," adds another.
Alabaster says nothing.

Once the other unicorns leave,
Alabaster sighs.
"What's the matter?" Hayley asks.
"Nothing," he mumbles.
The fairies look at one another with concern.

"You must want to talk to your parents,"
Abigail says.

"Yeah," Alabaster says, kicking the dirt.

"We should head home," Crystal says. "But
we'll see you tomorrow."

Early the next morning, there is a knock at the Weather Fairies' door.
It is Alabaster's parents.

"Alabaster is missing," Lady Gray says. "We think he's upset about moving."
"We can't find him in this mist," Quicksilver explains. "Can you help?"

"Yes," the fairies say together.

"He would never go far," Crystal insists. "He knows it isn't safe."

"We know all his hiding places," Evie tells them. "We'll find him."

The Weather Fairies fly over the foggy forest and land in the glen.

Evie swirls her wand, and the mist lifts.

Goldie twirls her wand, and the sun comes out. "That should shed some light on things," she says.

They look in Alabaster's favorite hide-and-seek spots, but they cannot find him.

"Alabaster!" the fairies call. "Come out, come out, wherever you are."

"Look! Behind that tree," Pearl declares. The fairies peek around the tree and see their friend.

"Alabaster, we're so glad we found you!"
Crystal says.
"Your parents are worried about you," Goldie
tells him.
"They said you are sad about moving,"
Pearl adds.
"I am," Alabaster sighs. "I'll miss my herd.
And I'll especially miss all of you."

"We'll miss you, too. But we'll still see you,"
Abigail says. "We're best friends."
"Promise?" Alabaster asks.
"Promise," the Weather Fairies reply.

The fairies walk Alabaster back to the herd.
His parents are happy and relieved to
see him.

"I'm sorry I ran off," Alabaster says.
"We're glad you are safe," says his father.

The king and queen join them.
"We hope you will enjoy living at the palace,
Alabaster," says the king.

"I think you will especially like the gardens," adds the queen. "They are wonderful for hide-and-seek."

"Hide-and-seek?" Alabaster says hopefully. The queen smiles and nods her head.

The Weather Fairies circle around Alabaster
and give him a hug.

"We'll miss you so much," Abigail says.

"Will you visit me soon?" Alabaster asks.

"Of course. We're best friends," Evie says.

"Ready or not, here we come!"

A Fairy Ballet

To Violet,
the superhero of fairy princess ballerinas.

With special thanks to Kristin Earhart

Pearl
the Cloud Fairy

Abigail
the Breeze Fairy

The Weather Fairies

Goldie
the Sunshine Fairy

Hayley
the Rain Fairy

Crystal
the Snow Fairy

Storm
the Lightning Fairy

Evie
the Mist Fairy

A Fairy Ballet

By Daisy Meadows

It's early morning in Fairyland, and the Weather Fairies are just waking up. There's a loud knock at their door. "Who could it be?" Crystal wonders.

Storm opens the door, and a frog strides in.
It's Bertram, the royal messenger.

"Hello, Weather Fairies," Bertram says.
"I have an invitation from the Fairy
Godmother for you."
"The Fairy Godmother?" gasps Evie.

Goldie opens the envelope and reads:

Dear fairies and friends:
Come one, come all!
In Fairyland, we will have a ball.
With songs and skits
for the king and queen,
it will be a celebration
like you've never seen.
Please be sure to prepare your part.
Bring a gift straight from your heart.
It's a night of fun for all to share.
I hope that I will see you there.

Always,
Fairy Godmother

"Oh, it sounds wonderful," sighs Hayley.
"But what about the gift?" Abigail asks.

"The Fairy Godmother wants the guests to
perform for the king and queen," Bertram
explains. "That will be your gift. Remember,
it needs to be from the heart."

The Weather Fairies look at one another.
"Have a good day," Bertram says. "See you at
the party."

"I can't believe we have to perform for the king and queen," says Crystal.

"We'll think of something," Goldie says.

"It has to be from the heart," Hayley reminds them.

Just then, a beautiful song dances
through the window.
"Let's go outside," suggests Crystal.
"We do our best thinking there."

Outside, the fairies see a bird.
"Was that your pretty song?" Pearl asks
the bird.

The bird chirps and flies toward the forest.
The fairies follow.

"I love to hear the breeze whisper," Abigail says.
"I love how things look magical in the mist,"
says Evie.

"Well, *I* love snowflakes," says Crystal.
"When I watch them whirl around, I want
to dance."
"We all love weather," Goldie says.
"Maybe that can be our gift."

"How?" asks Storm.

"We can dance to show everyone how weather makes us feel," says Goldie.

"We can create a ballet!" Evie exclaims.

All the fairies are excited, except Crystal.

"I'm not so sure," Crystal says quietly.

"But why?" Storm asks. "You love to dance."

"I like to dance for me," Crystal explains.

"But what if I mess up?"

"You'll be fine," Goldie insists.

"We'll practice. We're all in this together."
Crystal tries to smile.

Each fairy plans a special dance for her kind of weather.
Then they all work on the grand dance that comes at the end of their ballet.

"We're all in the finale," Hayley says. "Because it's a gift from all of us."

The fairies start to practice.

They help one another with their dances.
Each one is different, but they all tell a story
about weather.

When it is Crystal's turn, she is nervous.
Before her big leap, she stumbles and falls.

"I'll never get it right," Crystal says with a
sigh. "I can't dance in front of the king and
queen."

Abigail helps the snow fairy up.
"Don't worry about them," Evie suggests.
"When you dance from the heart, you
won't even know the crowd is there."

"I've seen you do that leap hundreds of
times," Hayley says. "You just have to
believe in yourself, like we believe in you."
Crystal nods and starts her dance again.

The Weather Fairies practice and practice.
They also design and sew their costumes.

Then they meet with the fairy orchestra.
A ballet needs music!

The night of the Fairy Godmother's party arrives.
There is a big outdoor stage.

The guests sit on blankets under the stars.
The Fairy Godmother, King Oberon, and
Queen Titania are there.

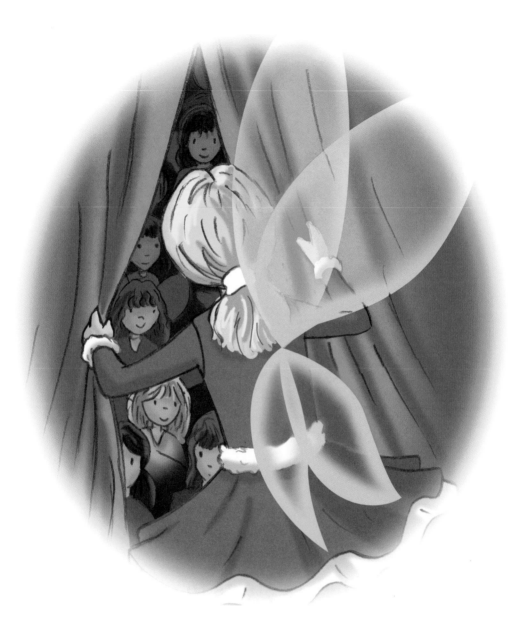

The Weather Fairies wait for their turn
backstage.
Crystal peeks out from behind the curtain
and crosses her wings for good luck.

The fairy orchestra starts to play the
ballet music.

Goldie is the first to go on. She does a
dance of the rising sun. At first, the stage is
dark. Then rays of light burst from Goldie's
wand as she dances.

Pearl bounds in next, flipping from one fluffy cloud to another.

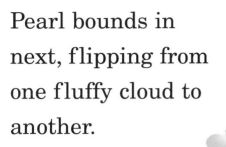

Storm's dance is like lightning: bold, fast, and flashy.

Hayley wears rain boots and dances with an umbrella, twirling in a dizzy spin.

Then Evie dances onto the stage, slow and graceful, like a misty dream.

Abigail wears a crown of acorns, and skips as she throws leaves in the air like the autumn breeze.

The music grows soft.
Giant, glittery snowflakes begin to fall.
Crystal floats onto the stage, whirling
around with the snowflakes.

It's time for her big jump. Crystal leaps
into the air. When she lands, she's so
happy, she glows.

The seven fairies dance onto the stage for the finale.
Their wings sparkle under the starry sky.

The music fills their hearts, and they
pirouette around the stage.
With a swirl of their wands, the sky
lights up with weather magic!

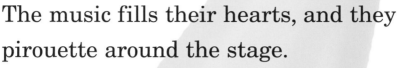

The Weather Fairies bow, and the Fairy Godmother hurries onto the stage. "What a beautiful ballet!" she exclaims. "We did it!" Goldie says to her fairy sisters. Crystal smiles. "Yes, we danced straight from the heart."

A Fairy
Treasure Hunt

To Neala Frances,
who loves a treasure hunt.

With special thanks to Kristin Earhart

Chloe
the Topaz Fairy

Amy
the Amethyst Fairy

The
Jewel
Fairies

Scarlett
the Garnet Fairy

India
the Moonstone
Fairy

Sophie
the Sapphire
Fairy

Emily
the Emerald Fairy

Lucy
the Diamond Fairy

A Fairy
Treasure Hunt

By Daisy Meadows

The morning sun shines on Fairyland.
The Jewel Fairies are excited.
"I can't believe today is the day!" says India.

"Our Fairy Test is finally here," Sophie agrees. "We've been training for so long."

Sophie looks around the cottage at
her sisters.
They are all fairies in training.
Once they pass their Fairy Test, they
will be full fairies.

"I wonder what our challenge will be,"
Sophie says.
"There's only one way to find out,"
says Emily.

After breakfast, the fairies fly
to the royal meadow.

As soon as they arrive, sparkles swirl in the sky. Queen Titania lands in front of them.

"Welcome to your Fairy Test," the queen says. "Your challenge will be a treasure hunt!"

"I will hide each of your jewels somewhere in
Fairyland," the queen explains.
She twirls her wand, and the seven gems
magically appear.

"Believe in yourselves and help one another
find the jewels," she says.
Then the colorful gems disappear right
before the fairies' eyes.

"Find your seven jewels and you will pass the test."

The queen smiles at the young fairies.

"Soon we'll be full fairies!" Sophie whispers to herself.

"Remember, the magic is inside you," the
queen says. "Good luck, Jewel Fairies!"
The wise fairy twirls her wand and
disappears.

"Where should we start?" Emily asks.

"She didn't give us any clues," Scarlett adds.

"Yes, she did," says India. "She said the magic is inside us."

"Maybe our magic will help us find our jewels," says Emily.

"But how?" asks Sophie.

"Just trust your magic," says India. "Come on!"
India grabs Sophie's hand, and all the Jewel Fairies fly into the air.
Their wings sparkle in the sunlight.

"I see something!" Chloe yells with delight.
"There are golden sparkles in that tree."
Chloe dives over for a closer look.
"My jewel is hiding in a bird's nest," she says.

The fairies split up to search for the
other gems.
India follows a trail of pale pink sparkles
into the castle.
"My moonstone was under the queen's pillow!"
she says with a giggle.

Amy and Scarlett see sparkles in the royal garden.
Scarlett finds her red jewel in the strawberry patch.
Amy's purple jewel is in a lilac bush.

Sophie searches the palace grounds, but she does not see blue sparkles anywhere.

"Look how the fountain glitters," Lucy says.
"It must be fairy magic."

Lucy zips down and plucks her jewel from
the top of the fountain.
"Hooray!" she exclaims.

The fairies fly to the Fairyland Forest.
Sophie and Emily are still looking for
their gems.

Emily spies a swirl of green sparkles coming from a hole in an old log.
She peeks inside.

"Well, hello there!" Emily says to a rabbit
family. "Thank you for keeping my jewel safe."
Emily gives each rabbit a pat.
Then she takes her green gem.

"We only have to find one more jewel," Chloe
says.

The fairies turn to Sophie.

"I haven't seen blue sparkles anywhere,"
Sophie says. "Maybe I don't have any magic
inside me."

"You just need to believe in yourself," says Amy.
"What's your favorite part of being a fairy?"
Scarlett asks.
Sophie thinks for a moment. "I love to make
wishes come true," she says.

"Maybe you need to make your own wish now," Emily suggests.

Sophie takes a deep breath. "I'll try. Will you help me?" she asks.

The sisters nod and form a circle.

Sophie recites her wish. It sounds like a song.

"Magic might, magic may,
Be with us this very day.
In a circle fairies bow,
May magic grant my wish right now."

The fairies touch their wands together.
A burst of blue sparkles appears.

"Look, the sparkles make a path," India says.
The Jewel Fairies follow the trail.

"The sparkles lead through here," says Sophie
as she pushes back some leafy branches.
Sophie gasps with surprise.

Queen Titania is standing in the clearing, and she has Sophie's blue jewel in her hands!

"Congratulations on finishing the treasure hunt!" the queen exclaims. "You found all the jewels. This calls for a celebration!"

Now the fairy sisters are full fairies.
The queen gives them necklaces.
Hanging from each necklace is the special
jewel each fairy found.

"This has been a magical day," says India.
"Yes," Sophie agrees. "It's been like a wish
come true!"

A
Fairyland
Costume Ball

To Rosie,
who is full of surprises.

With special thanks to Kristin Earhart

Chloe
the Topaz Fairy

Amy
the Amethyst Fairy

The Jewel Fairies

Scarlett
the Garnet Fairy

India
the Moonstone
Fairy

Sophie
the Sapphire
Fairy

Lucy
the Diamond Fairy

Emily
the Emerald Fairy

A Fairyland Costume Ball

By Daisy Meadows

Red leaves drop from the trees.
It is fall in Fairyland.

Halloween will be here soon.
The Jewel Fairies are excited.

Halloween is a magical time in Fairyland. The fairy king and queen always throw a grand costume ball.

All the fairies dress up, dance, and celebrate. The Jewel Fairies want their costumes to be extra special.

Flora the Dress-up Fairy and Trixie the Halloween Fairy arrive at the Jewel Fairies' cottage.

They want to help their friends get ready for
the ball.

Flora swirls her wand, and all kinds of
costumes appear.

"Halloween is fun because you can dress up however you want!" says Trixie.

"Let's all look for costumes that match the color of our jewels," Sophie suggests.
"What a colorful idea!" Chloe agrees.

Amy searches through racks of dresses and stacks of masks, but she doesn't find anything special.

"What's wrong, Amy?" asks Trixie.
"I can't find the right costume for the ball,"
she explains.

"Do you want to look fancy? Silly? Scary?"
Trixie asks.

"I don't know," Amy admits. "I want to
surprise everyone."
"Hmmm." Trixie sighs. "We'll think of
something."

Finally, it's Halloween night.
The Jewel Fairies chat and laugh as they
get ready.

Scarlett puts on her tiara.
Sophie paints whiskers on Chloe.

Lucy puts on a snowy headband.
"You look delicious!" India tells Emily.

Amy is in the corner with Trixie.
"What are you up to?" Chloe asks.

"Trixie is helping me put the last touches on
my costume," Amy says with a sly smile.
"What costume?" asks Scarlett.
"You'll see," Amy replies.

Finally, it is time to leave.

"Has anyone seen Amy?" India asks.

"It's like she disappeared," Emily says.

"She told me that she will meet you at the ball," Trixie explains.

With hats and crowns and masks and makeup, the fairies set out for the costume ball.

"Let's take a shortcut through the Enchanted Forest," says Sophie. "It's faster."
"And spookier," Scarlett adds.

The shadows are long and dark in the forest.
A low moan echoes through the trees.

Scarlett shivers. "What was that?" she asks.
"I'm sure it was just the wind," Emily says,
but her voice trembles.

The fairies look around.
They don't see anyone.
They hear the low moan again.

OOOOOOO, OOOOOOOOOO

"It sounds like a ghost!" Lucy cries. She
grabs India's hand.

The fairies feel a chill as the air rushes around them.

"I'm worried about Amy," Sophie says. "She will be walking all alone."

At last, the Jewel Fairies reach the
Fairyland Palace.
It twinkles in the moonlight.
"It looks beautiful!" says Chloe.

"Let's hurry," Lucy says. "The ball is about to begin."

When they enter the palace, Queen
Titania spots the Jewel Fairies.
"Welcome," she says. "But where is Amy?"

Just then, they hear the low moan again.

OOOOOOO, OOOOOOOOOO

A burst of purple sparkles appears.
"Boo! I'm a ghost!"

The Jewel Fairies shriek with surprise.
They know that voice.
It's Amy!

"You scared us!" Scarlett declares.
"You really didn't know it was me?" Amy asks.
"Not at all. That's a terrific costume," Flora tells Amy.

"I made it myself," Amy says, "with a little magic, of course!"

"Now we're all here! Let's have some Halloween fun," India says.

The Jewel Fairies join in the festivities.

Emily and Scarlett bob for apples.

Amy and Chloe eat pumpkin cupcakes.

All the fairies dance the Monster Mash.

At midnight, it's time for a special toast.
The Jewel Fairies raise their punch glasses.
"Happy Halloween!" announce the king
and queen.

Amy clinks her glass. "Here's to another
magical year filled with surprises!"